PEER GYNT

~Retold by Wynne Birbeck~

~Illustrated by Ian Deuchar~

Collins Educational

Contents

CHAPTER 1

Peer Gynt steals the bride

Have you sometimes wished you could get things without having to work for them? Peer Gynt was like that all the time. Not just now and then – ALL THE TIME. He wasn't just lazy, he was selfish too.

He lived with his mother, in a tiny wooden house at the edge of a village in Norway.

His mother worked very hard. She cooked and washed and scrubbed and dusted. Then she went to other houses to do the same. People paid her to do their very hard work. Peer had no job at all. He sat about the house, dreaming of making a fortune. Sometimes he went for walks on his own in the forest. When he came home, he was hungry, but he did not make any meals. Instead, he was angry if his mother had not finished cooking for him. Sometimes, he even shouted at her.

One evening, Peer got home before his mother. He was very hungry, but he did not try to make a meal.

When his mother came in, looking very tired. Peer greeted her by shouting, 'Where have you been? I'm hungry and you were not here to cook for me.'

This time, Peer's mother shouted back. 'You lazy young man!' she cried. 'I have been working all day, as usual, while you have been doing nothing. Walking in the forest will not earn your fortune. No wonder no-one wants to be your friend. You are too selfish and lazy.'

This made Peer even more angry. He stamped his foot. 'I don't care if no-one likes me,' he shouted. 'I think everyone is stupid'

His mother looked sad. 'Peer', she said, 'if you don't mend your ways, you will live your life all alone and be very, very sad.'

At that moment, there was a knock at the door. Peer's mother opened it. There stood a young man in a very smart uniform. He held out a letter.

'Please will you reply straight away?' asked the young man.

'Come in,' said Peer's mother, as she opened the letter.

'What is it? What is it?' asked Peer excitedly.

It was an invitation from the richest man in the village. He was inviting everyone to his daughter's wedding.

'What! Even me?' asked Peer.

'My master said everyone,' replied the young man.

Peer's mother agreed to go, but only if Peer promised not to be rude to everyone.

'I promise I'll be good. Really I will,' said Peer.

The party was a very grand one. Everyone was dressed in their best clothes. The bride was marrying a rich young man, and Peer felt very jealous. When the dancing began, Peer stood alone. He knew people didn't like him, so he didn't ask anyone to dance with him.

He was very surprised when a pretty girl came up to him and asked if he would like to dance with her.

'Do you know who I am?' asked Peer.

'Yes,' replied the girl.

'And you still want to dance with me?'

'Of course I do, or I wouldn't have asked you.'

Peer was delighted. As they danced, and talked, Peer found out that the girl's name was Solveig. He liked her very much.

Suddenly a cross-looking woman came over and grabbed Solveig's arm.

'Do you really want to dance with HIM?' asked the woman. She was Solveig's mother.

'Yes,' said Solveig.

'Well, I don't want you to. Come along,' said her mother, and she began to pull Solveig away.

Solveig looked sadly back at Peer as she followed her mother.

Peer was absolutely furious.

'That does it.' he shouted.

As everyone turned away from him, he caught sight of the bride standing near him.

'I'll show all of you,' he shouted, and he grabbed the bride's arm and dragged her with him as he ran from the room.

'Oh, my goodness,' said Solveig's mother, 'Peer Gynt has stolen the bride.'

CHAPTER 2

The trolls' cave

Peer didn't wait to see if anyone followed. He ran and ran. All the time he held onto the bride's hand, so she had to run with him.

They ran out of the village and into the forest – deep, deep into the forest.

At last they stopped, exhausted.

Peer Gynt looked at the bride. She was frightened, but she was angry, too.

'I hate you!' she cried. 'I want to go home.'

'Go on, then,' said Peer. 'Go away. I don't like you, either.'

'As the bride set off to find her way back, she shouted, 'I hope the trolls get you.'

'I don't believe in those stupid little people,' said Peer. crossly.

Sitting on a log, Peer put his head in his hands. 'Why did I do that?' he asked himself. 'What am I going to do now?'

A voice behind him called out 'Peer Gynt.' And then louder, 'PEER GYNT!' He turned and saw a strange woman dressed all in green. Even her skin looked a greenish colour.

'Who are you?' asked Peer.

'Never mind who I am,' said the Green Woman. 'I know who you are, and that is what is important. I've been watching you for a long time. It's time you joined some people who will appreciate you.'

'Do you mean they could help me make my fortune?' asked Peer.

The Green Woman smiled a secret smile. 'You could say that,' she replied.

'Then lead the way,' cried Peer.

Peer followed the Green Woman deeper and deeper into the forest. The trees grew very close together, so it was dark and gloomy. The ground was steep and rocky.

At last, she stopped, and pointed to a very large hole in some big rocks. 'Go through the entrance and wait,' said the Green Woman. Again she smiled her secret smile.

Peer walked carefully through the opening. He found himself in a cave. It was dark and damp, and he seemed to hear strange music coming from far away. Suddenly, he was surrounded by fierce, dancing little people, who poked and prodded at him with long, bony fingers. Wild music seemed to fill the whole cave.

Peer was pushed and grabbed. First one way, then another. He was afraid. He wanted to shout out, but all he could think was 'TROLLS!' Perhaps the Green Woman had granted the bride's wish.

The dancers whirled and jumped about him. They were dancing nearer and nearer to him.

Suddenly, a bell rang out somewhere. It sounded like the church bell in the village. It rang and rang.

The music stopped. The dancers stopped. They put their hands over their ears because they hated the church bell.

Peer remembered that he had heard long ago that trolls could not bear the sound of church bells. It hurt their ears because they were so wicked.

Soon, all the trolls disappeared from the cave.

He did not wait for them to return. He rushed outside and began to run back through the forest.

At last he stopped. He could go no further. He sank down onto the pine needles beneath a great, tall tree, and soon he was fast asleep. He was woken by someone shaking him gently.

Opening his eyes, he saw Solveig. She was very glad to see him safe. She told him that it was she who had rung the church bell. 'I heard the trolls were out in the mountains and forest, and I was worried about you,' she said.

Solveig had saved Peer's life. He felt that he would like to stay with her forever. He remembered what his mother had said about him. He promised he would work very hard to look after Solveig and himself, and so she agreed to stay with him, living in the forest.

Peer made them a little wooden house to live in.

CHAPTER 3

Peer Gynt's travels

Time passed and Peer was very happy with his new life. Sometimes he still wished he could make his fortune easily, but he wanted to take care of Solveig so he worked hard.

One day, as he was in the forest chopping wood, he was surprised to meet the Green Woman again.

Remembering the trolls, he did not want to stop and talk at first. The Green Woman smiled her secret smile and said, 'Don't you still want to make your fortune, Peer Gynt?'

'Well, I'd like to, but I must look after Solveig,' said Peer.

'Why?' asked the Green Woman in a low voice.

As soon as she said it, Peer began to ask himself the same question.

Very quickly, he forgot all about looking after Solveig. In fact, he forgot about everything but making his fortune.

He followed the Green Woman as she led him away through the deep forest. And so began his journeys to strange places.

The Green Woman finally left Peer Gynt near a ship, at a busy port. He could not remember how he got there.

He decided to travel on the ship to seek his fortune. He had just enough money to pay for his journey to the ship's first port of call. After that, he had to work as a sailor to earn his way. It was very hard work and Peer didn't like it at all. No-one spoke much to him.

As he worked, he listened to the other sailors talking. He heard about many ways he could make lots of money. He liked best the ones which meant he didn't have to work hard. He decided to leave the ship and try out some of the ideas.

The first land he visited was very, very hot and it hardly ever rained. Most of the countryside was a sandy desert.

At first, Peer made some money by buying and selling things. But he had really come to this hot land because he had heard that he could make lots of money very quickly there, by buying and selling PEOPLE.

Peer was now only interested in getting rich. He had forgotten all about Solveig. He was even prepared to do something very wicked to make money. He bought some slaves and then sold them to a wealthy man for a lot of money.

He stayed at the wealthy man's house and there he met a beautiful dancer called Anitra. Like Solveig, Anitra liked Peer. She offered to help him find a new home, so that he could stay with her in this hot desert land.

She tried very hard to make him stay. She even danced a special dance for him. Peer thanked her, but he did not stay. He began to remember Solveig. But then he thought that he could make even more money if he travelled on. It was already four years since he had last seen Solveig.

Poor Solveig! At first she could not believe that Peer had gone away. Every day she walked in the forest looking for him. She spent her time alone, singing a sad little song, and hoping that Peer would soon come home to her. And so the days went by and became months and years, and Solveig was no longer young. Still she waited for Peer.

Meanwhile, Peer travelled far and wide, seeing many strange sights, meeting many people, but never making any friends. It was just as his mother had warned – he was alone. More and more, as he grew older, he thought about Solveig and their little wooden house in the forest. He had indeed made lots of money, but he, too, was no longer young. Perhaps Solveig would not recognize him with his beard and his grey hair.

At last, he decided to end his travels.

CHAPTER 4

Home at last

Peer Gynt boarded a tall ship taking with him things to sell in Norway. At least he had stopped selling people.

On the first night at sea, a great storm arose, and the ship was tossed and blown about.

Suddenly, a great bolt of lightning struck the side of the ship and made a huge hole. Water rushed in, and soon the ship began to sink. Peer was thrown into the water. He was sure he would drown. He wished with all his heart he had never left his dear Solveig. He wanted more than anything to see her.

As he grew tired, he found it harder and harder to swim. Suddenly, he saw a big basket floating near him. It must have come from the ship. He caught hold of it. It kept him afloat and alive.

When at last Peer reached the shore, it was not Norway. And all his fortune was left behind, at the bottom of the sea. After all his lonely travels, here he was – on his way home, no richer than the day he left. He could not afford to travel by coach or ship to Norway, and so he set off to travel the only way he could. He walked. Sometimes he was helped on his journey by kind people who gave him food or shelter. One man even gave him some new shoes when his old ones wore out.

The journey took Peer many weeks, for he was now quite an old man. He travelled more slowly now than he had on that day, long ago, when he had followed the Green Woman. At last he found himself at the edge of his own dear forest.

He looked around with pleasure. The trees were green and tall. The birds sang. Peer's heart felt light and happy. This was strange, for he had nothing to bring back from his travels. He had lost all his fortune in the sea.

At last he came to the little wooden house. It was just as he had remembered it.

But who was that elderly lady sitting outside in the sun, gently rocking in her chair and singing?

Suddenly Peer realised that, just as he had become older, so had Solveig. He had forgotten how many years had gone by. He hoped she would be glad to see him again. 'Solveig,' he called.

The woman stopped singing and turned to look at him. He waved, and called her name again.

A look of great joy filled the old woman's face. She stood up slowly and began to walk towards him. Peer walked towards her as fast as he could.

They reached each other in the middle of the garden. They looked at each other and then they both smiled. Peer put his arms around Solveig, and she hugged him tight.

'Oh Solveig,' said Peer, 'how much I've missed you. I see now my mother was right about me. How I wish I could tell her, but it's too late. All I can do is make sure I look after you better. Now I know that the most important thing in life is to have someone to love.'